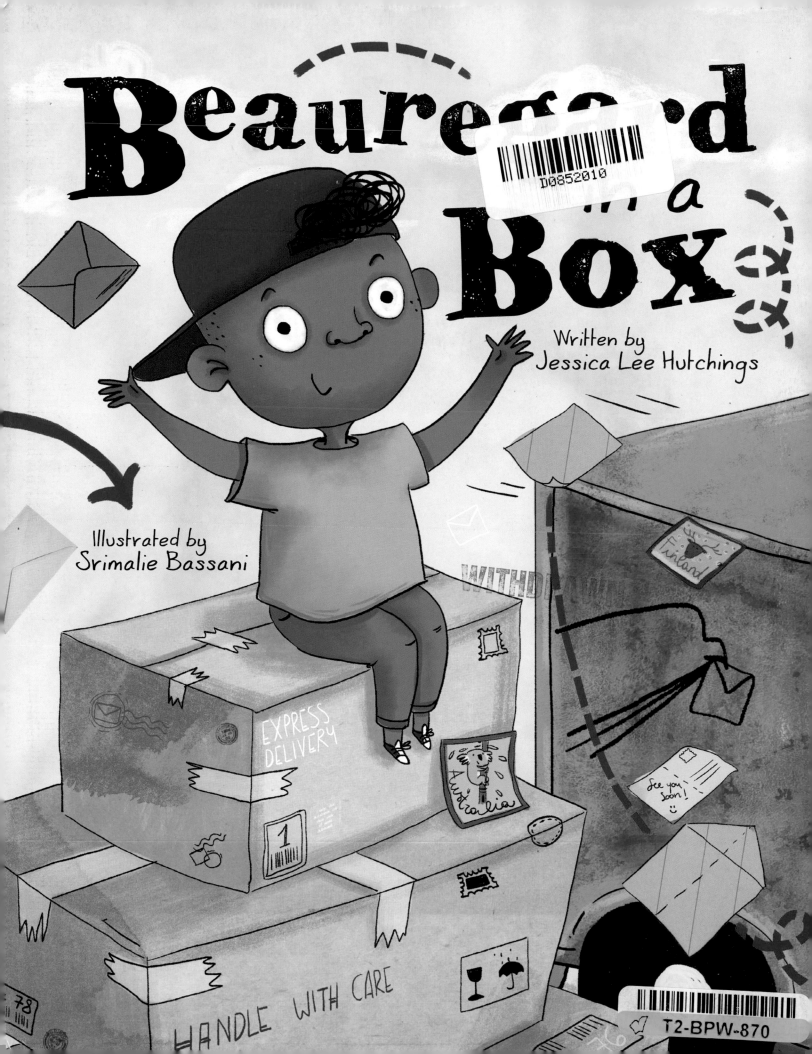

ARCTIC
OCEAN

PACIFIC
OCEAN

ATLANTIC
OCEAN

SOUTHERN

INDIAN

OCEAN

OCEAN

Beauregard had big dreams all night and all day
of visiting people and worlds far, far away.
He would dream and he'd think. He would read, draw, and write.
And all of that thinking kept him up late at night!

In his dreams he would travel the whole world around,
but in real life he preferred to stay safe on the ground.
He was scared of airplanes. He was scared of big boats.
"That huge thing that flies?! That monster that floats?!
Those things all scare me and I don't like fear.
I'll just stay in Alabama; I'm much safer here!"

And so he just kept on dreaming. He would read, draw, and write about a grand ocean trip or an overseas flight.

Then one day Beauregard came up with a plan,
while looking outside at the yellow mail van.
Inside the mail van was a mega-huge crate.
"Hmmmmmmmmmmmmmmmmmmm...
something like that there would fit me just great!"

He sketched out a plan and worked through the night—
he would travel the world without taking a flight!
He got himself ready with all he would need,
then set out not knowing where this grand plan would lead.

He found the post office and was ready to go!
He snuck around back and through a window.

He saw a huge box and he crawled right inside.
It was packed full of mittens. What a great place to hide!

BWING!

CLANG!

BONG!

BANG!

BING!

CLING!

"It's dark, it's noisy, I can't see a thing!"

When the box had arrived at its addressed destination,
Beau peeked out to discover his current location.

"Hei!" came a voice from outside the box.
"I'm Aleksi," said a boy with thick, fuzzy socks.
"Welcome to Finland, I hope you like snow!"
Beauregard was in shock but his face just said,
"Ohhhhhhhhhhhhhhhhhhh..."

Finland

Lapland

Helsinki

"I'll take you around and show you the sights:
the ice hotel, the reindeer, the bright northern lights."
So Beau and Aleksi went all over town,
sledding and skiing and exploring around.

Beauregard loved Finland, but wanted to roam.
"There is much more to see before I head home!"
As he waved bye to Aleksi, he saw a box in a shop
and was excited to see what would be his next stop!

He strolled up to the box and then crawled right inside.
It was full of sarongs. What a great place to hide!

BWING!
CLANG!

BONG!
BANG!
BING!
CLING!

"It's dark, it's noisy, I can't see a thing!"

When the box had arrived at its addressed destination,
Beau peeked out to discover his current location.

"Om suastiastu!" came a voice from outside.
"I'm Sinta," said a girl as she smiled with pride.
"Welcome to Bali, I hope you like sun!"
Beauregard was surprised but he just yelled out,
"Fuuuuuuuuuuuuuuuuuuun!"

"I'll take you around and show you the sights:
volcanoes, monkeys, and island delights."
So Beau followed Sinta exploring around
and surfing the waves with the new friend he'd found.

Denpasar

Nusa Penida

Beau just loved Bali, but felt ready for more.
The world seemed full of nice people and adventures galore!
He waved bye to Sinta and found a box drop,
excited to see what would be his next stop!

He picked a large carton and crawled right inside.
It was loaded with swimsuits. What a great place to hide!

When the box had arrived at its addressed destination,
Beau peeked out to discover his current location.

"G'day!" came a voice from outside like before.
"I'm Jack," said a boy standing at his front door.
"Welcome to Oz, I hope you like heat!"
Beau said, "Australia?! Man, that is so
sweeeeeeeeeeeeeeeeeeeet!"

"I'll take you 'round here and show you the roos,
koalas, wallabies, didgeridoos."
So Beauregard and Jack would hoot, holler, and shout,
as they swam and explored on a long walkabout.

Australia

It was soon time to get home.
Beau told Jack he must leave.
"Check out this great trick I've got up my sleeve."
As he waved bye to Jack, he climbed into a crate,
but Jack looked perplexed and he yelled out, "Beau, **WAIT!**"

"You're heading for home packed into that crate?
It's dark, it's noisy, and the ride can't be great!"

Beauregard felt silly and shrugged with a frown.
"How else can I travel back to my hometown?"

"A plane!" said Jack with a smile big and bright.
But Beauregard's face clouded over with fright.

"How do you think your box got all this way?
You flew on a plane, just hidden away!
Besides, think of all the cool stuff you have done!
Exploring the world! The friends and the fun!
You're brave, Beauregard!" Jack loudly proclaimed.
"You are a brave enough kid to fly home on a plane!"

So Beau thought it over and realized it was true!
He'd done one brave thing, so why not try two?

Beauregard is now back home in sweet Alabama
with his friends and his family and even his grandma!
These days when he dreams about worlds far away,
his thoughts are of people he met on the way.
He thinks of Aleksi, Sinta, and Jack
and imagines the day when he can go back.

He knows there are many more places to see.
And he says, "I can do it. No one is braver than
meeeeeeeeeeeeeeeeeeee!"

ARCTIC OCEAN

PACIFIC OCEAN

ATLANTIC OCEAN

SOUTHERN